RESCUING THE PLATED LIZARD

Other books in the series:

Attack of the
LIZARD KING

Charge of the
THREE-HORNED MONSTER

March of the
ARMOURED BEASTS

Flight of the
WINGED SERPENT

Catching the
SPEEDY THIEF

Stampede of the
GIANT REPTILES

Swimming with the
SEA MONSTER

DINOSAUR COVE™

RESCUING THE PLATED LIZARD

by
REX STONE

illustrated by
MIKE SPOOR

Series created by
Working Partners Ltd

OXFORD
UNIVERSITY PRESS

Special thanks to Jane Clarke

To Susan – a great mother, loving sister and
best friend - R.S

To Christopher - M.S

OXFORD
UNIVERSITY PRESS

Great Clarendon Street, Oxford OX2 6DP
Oxford University Press is a department of the University of Oxford.
It furthers the University's objective of excellence in research, scholarship,
and education by publishing worldwide in

Oxford   New York

Auckland   Cape Town   Dar es Salaam   Hong Kong   Karachi
Kuala Lumpur   Madrid   Melbourne   Mexico City   Nairobi
New Delhi   Shanghai   Taipei   Toronto

With offices in

Argentina   Austria   Brazil   Chile   Czech Republic   France   Greece
Guatemala   Hungary   Italy   Japan   Poland   Portugal   Singapore
South Korea   Switzerland   Thailand   Turkey   Ukraine   Vietnam

Oxford is a registered trade mark of Oxford University Press
in the UK and in certain other countries

British Library Cataloguing in Publication Data

Data available

ISBN: 978-0-19-272836-4

1 3 5 7 9 10 8 6 4 2

Printed in Great Britain by CPI Cox & Wyman, Reading, RG1 8EX
Paper used in the production of this book is a natural,
recyclable product made from wood grown in sustainable forests
The manufacturing process conforms to the environmental
regulations of the country of origin

FACT FILE

▷ JAMIE AND HIS BEST FRIEND TOM HAVE DISCOVERED A SECRET CAVE WITH FOSSILIZED DINOSAUR FOOTPRINTS AND, WHEN THEY PLACE THEIR FEET OVER EACH OF THE FOSSILS IN TURN, THEY ARE MAGICALLY TRANSPORTED TO A WORLD WITH REAL, LIVE DINOSAURS. THEY'VE HAD A TON OF ADVENTURES WITH THEIR DINOSAUR FRIEND WANNA, MEETING DINOSAURS FROM THE LATE CRETACEOUS, BUT WHAT ABOUT DINOSAURS FROM THE OTHER TIME PERIODS?

JAMIE

- **FULL NAME:** JAMIE MORGAN
- **AGE:** 8 YEARS
- **SIZE:** 1 JATOM*
- **TOP SPEED:** 10 KPH
- **LIKES:** FOSSIL HUNTING AND LEARNING ABOUT DINOSAURS
- **DISLIKES:** BEING STUCK INDOORS

Jamie's eye

Jamie's foot

Jamie's hand

*NOTE: A JATOM IS THE SIZE OF JAMIE OR TOM: 125 CM TALL AND 27 KG IN WEIGHT

TOM

- **FULL NAME:** THOMAS CLAY
- **AGE:** 8 YEARS
- **SIZE:** 1 JATOM*
- **TOP SPEED:** 10 KPH
- **LIKES:** TRACKING ANIMALS AND EXPLORING WILDLIFE
- **DISLIKES:** RAINY DAYS

Tom's eye

Tom's hand

WANNA

- **FULL NAME:** WANNANOSAURUS
- **AGE:** 65 – 80 MILLION YEARS**
- **SIZE:** LESS THAN A JATOM*
- **TOP SPEED:** 50 KPH, ESPECIALLY WHEN BEING CHASED BY A T-REX
- **LIKES:** STINKY GINGKO FRUIT AND BANGING HIS HEAD ON TREE TRUNKS
- **DISLIKES:** SCARY DINOSAURS

Wanna's head

Wanna's foot

*NOTE: A JATOM IS THE SIZE OF JAMIE OR TOM: 125 CM TALL AND 27 KG IN WEIGHT
**NOTE: SCIENTISTS CALL THIS PERIOD THE LATE CRETACEOUS

STEGOSAURUS

Stegosaurus's eye

Stegosaurus's plate

Stegosaurus's foot

Stegosaurus's tail

- **FULL NAME:** STEGOSAURUS
- **AGE:** ABOUT 150 MILLION YEARS***
- **HEIGHT:** 3 JATOMS*
- **LENGTH:** 8 JATOMS*
- **WEIGHT:** 150 JATOMS*
- **LIKES:** MUNCHING ON FERNS AND SOAKING UP SUNSHINE
- **DISLIKES:** BEING TOLD IT HAS A BRAIN THE SIZE OF A WALNUT.

*NOTE: A JATON IS THE SIZE OF JAMIE OR TOM: 125 CM TALL AND 27 KG IN WEIGHT
***NOTE: SCIENTISTS CALL THIS PERIOD THE JURASSIC

DINOSAUR COVE

Village

Marina

Sealight Head

8

Landslips where clay and fossils are

Muddy beach

DINO CAVE

Tide beach line

Low Tide beach line

Sea

Smuggler's Point

CHAPTER 1

'Dino World here we come!'

Jamie Morgan and his best friend, Tom Clay, clattered down the stairs of the old lighthouse ready for a new adventure. They burst into the museum on the ground floor and skidded to a halt in front of Jamie's dad.

'It's good to hear you being so enthusiastic about the museum,' Jamie's dad said. He was kneeling on the floor beside a sandpit, arranging plastic trowels around the edge.

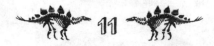

Jamie spluttered. 'Er um . . . it's awesome!' He hadn't been talking about his dad's fantastic dinosaur museum. He'd meant the secret world of real dinosaurs that he and Tom had discovered in a hidden cave.

'Visitors will love your new exhibit,' Tom said to change the subject. He took a trowel

and poked at a cookie-sized fossil half-buried in the sand. 'That's an ammonite.'

'If you dig it out and match it with the ammonites on display you can find out what time period it comes from,' Mr Morgan told him.

Jamie looked into the glass display case against the wall. Each ammonite fossil was carefully labelled with time periods, including Permian, Triassic, Jurassic, and Cretaceous.

Jamie started rummaging in his backpack. 'Can you tell when my ammonite is from?' he asked, pulling out the one he'd found on his first day on the beach in Dinosaur Cove.

Permian

Triassic

Jurassic

Cretaceous

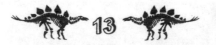

13

Jamie's dad studied the fossil closely and checked it against the ones in the display case. 'It has deep ridges and the ribs are complete circles around the outer edge. That means it's definitely Late Cretaceous.'

Jamie smiled at Tom. Their secret cave led to a world with real, live Late Cretaceous dinosaurs like triceratops and velociraptors.

'Ammonites are like keys to the past,' Jamie's dad went on. 'Scientists use them to help date the rock layers where they're found.'

'Cool,' Tom said.

'We're going exploring,' Jamie said. 'You can keep my ammonite for the exhibit.'

'Thanks, son.' Jamie's dad buried it under the sand with the other ammonites. 'Have fun!'

'We will.'

Jamie and Tom dashed out of the lighthouse and ran as fast as they could along the beach and up the cliff to the old smugglers' cave.

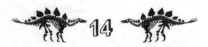

'I can't wait to see Wanna again,' Tom said as they wriggled through the gap at the back of the cave into the secret chamber. They'd met the wannanosaurus on their first trip to Dino World and the little dinosaur had been their friend ever since. It was actually their dinosaur friend's fossilized footprints that had transported them into Dino World.

'Any second now . . .' Jamie could feel the excitement bubbling up inside him as he put his feet into Wanna's fossilized footprints. What dinosaurs would they meet today?

'One, two, three . . .' Jamie headed towards the rock face. 'Four, five —OUCH!' Instead of emerging into Dino World, Jamie smacked into the solid rock.

Tom bumped into the back of him. 'What happened?'

Jamie rubbed his scraped knee. 'I don't know.' He shone his torch on the fossil footprints.

'You must be doing it wrong,' Tom said. 'Let me go first.' He took five confident steps and then his head whacked against the cave wall. 'OW!' he yelled, rubbing his forehead. 'It's not working!'

Jamie fought down a wave of panic. 'We must be doing something different.'

'We're walking like we always do and wearing what we always wear,' Tom said. 'What's in your backpack?'

Jamie tipped out the
contents and shone his torch on
them. 'Fossil Finder, compass, map,
binoculars, sandwiches.' He stuffed everything
back in.

'Even the sandwiches are the same—
cheese and your grandad's pickle.' Tom sighed.

'But something must have changed,' Jamie
insisted.

'Maybe something's missing,' Tom said.

'My ammonite!' Jamie jumped to his feet.
'It's been with us every time we've been to
Dino World. We've got to get it back!'

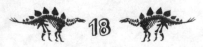

They raced to the old lighthouse and the main door was still shut. The museum hadn't yet opened for the day.

'We're in luck,' Tom said as Jamie pulled open the heavy door. They tiptoed into the museum and peered cautiously around.

'There's no sign of Dad. Quick!' Jamie and Tom each grabbed a trowel and dug in the sand. Soon, they each had a big pile of ammonites to look through.

'That's the lot.' Jamie put down his trowel and started looking through the fossils. 'My ammonite is black with shiny gold ridges, and it's about as big as a yo-yo.'

'We should put the wrong ones back,' Tom suggested.

'Good idea,' Jamie agreed. They reburied the fossils that were too big or too small or made of the wrong type of stone until only two were left.

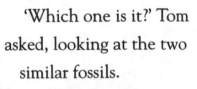

'Which one is it?' Tom asked, looking at the two similar fossils.

'It's hard to tell,' Jamie said, 'but I think it's this one.'

Tom agreed and Jamie stuffed the ammonite he was holding into his pocket whilst Tom pushed the other one back into the

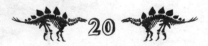

sandpit. They slipped out of the door and ran
back to the cave as fast as they could.

'Fingers crossed.' Jamie fitted his feet into
Wanna's fossilized footprints.
'One, two, three . . .'
He walked slowly towards
the wall, bracing himself
for impact with the solid
rock. 'Four . . .' Jamie
held his hands out in front
of him as he stepped
forward. 'Five!'

He felt a sudden rush of
hot, humid air and his ears
rang with the calls of strange
jungle creatures. He took a
deep breath and his nostrils
filled with the peaty
smell of warm leaf-
mould. Jamie opened

his eyes. Tom was standing next to him. They were back in Dino World.

'Hurrah!' Tom shouted.

Jamie looked behind him to check that their usual way home was there and was relieved to see the muddy version of the fossilized footprints leading away from the back of the cave.

'Everything is back to normal,' Jamie declared. 'Let's go!' Jamie and Tom dashed out of the cave and set off through the gingko trees.

Jamie parted the creepers and stopped dead. 'What happened to the view?'

Tom's mouth dropped open. 'I have no idea.'

The hillside view over the grassy plains, the winding river, Fang Rock, and Far Away Mountains had disappeared. Instead, all they could see was the trunks of more jungle trees. Dino World had changed!

CHAPTER 2

SEARCH:

'Where are we?' Tom asked.

'There's only one way to find out.' Jamie looked up for the tallest gingko tree, grabbed a low branch and swung himself up. Tom climbed on behind him. They hauled themselves up through the sturdy branches until they could see out over Dino World.

Tom wrapped his legs around a branch and looked through his binoculars. 'The lagoon is gone!' He gulped. 'And there are hills in the south-east where the marsh should be.'

'And the White
Ocean's a lot nearer,'
Jamie added, gazing
across the sea towards
the horizon. A dark

shape broke the surface of the bright
blue water.

'Pass me the binoculars.' Jamie hung
on to the tree trunk and focused on where
the creature had appeared. A crocodilian

head on the end of a snake-like neck came into view, followed by an elephant-sized grey-green body. The creature lay basking on the surface, lazily moving its four huge flippers.

'Cool!' Jamie declared. 'I'm glad we didn't catch anything like that when we went crabbing.' Jamie handed the binoculars back to Tom.

'We'd never have got it in the crab bucket.' Tom chuckled. He twisted round with the binoculars still to his eyes.

'The Plains are still there, but the Far Away Mountains aren't just mountains any more,' he said. 'They look like volcanoes.'

Tom handed the binoculars to Jamie and pushed his curly red hair behind his sticky-out ears. 'What's going on?' he asked.

Jamie slowly scanned the horizon. At the edge of the plains, a pair of long-necked

dinosaurs were grazing on the top branches of tall conifer trees.

'Brachiosaurs,' Jamie whispered. 'I thought they were from the Jurassic. I can't see *any* of the Cretaceous dinosaurs we usually see. No triceratops, no ankylosaurs, no T-Rex . . .'

Tom laughed. 'I'm glad about the last one!'

At the sound of Tom's laughter a pair of crow-sized creatures perching in the tree above them began squawking and flapping their electric blue feathers.

'They've got claws at the end of their wings,' Jamie said in surprise. 'And beaks full of tiny teeth,' Tom added. 'What are they?'

'I'll find out.' Jamie wedged himself between the trunk and the branch he was sitting on and took out his Fossil Finder. He typed *BIRD WITH TEETH AND CLAWS* into the search box.

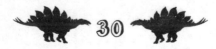

30

'ARCHAEOPTERYX,' Jamie read. 'PART BIRD AND PART DINOSAUR, DATING FROM THE JURASSIC PERIOD ABOUT A HUNDRED AND FIFTY MILLION YEARS AGO.' He snapped the Fossil Finder shut and shoved it into his backpack. 'You know what this means?'

Jamie and Tom looked at each other. 'We're in the Jurassic!' they yelled, holding on to the tree trunk with one hand and giving each other a high five with the other.

Jamie's heart leapt for joy. They'd arrived in a different time. They had a whole new Dino World to explore and a whole new set of dinosaurs to see!

CHAPTER 3

Jamie and Tom scrambled eagerly down the gingko tree and plunged into the steamy Jurassic jungle. A cloud of insects the size of paper aeroplanes, with long dangly legs, whirred into the air around them.

'Do Jurassic bugs have stings?' Jamie asked nervously, flapping his hands as he tried to keep them from settling on his head.

'I hope not!' Tom muttered. 'We need a Jurassic bug swat.' He wiped the sweat from his hands on his T-shirt, then tried to snap off

one of the stems of the horsetail
ferns that towered above
their heads. He bent and
twisted it but the thick,
jointed rod-like stem
refused to break.

'These ferns are really
tough,' he muttered.

'Here.' Jamie tore off a couple
of smaller fronds and handed one
to Tom. They swished at the
insects as they pushed on through
the jungle.

'So, how did we come out of
the cave into a different time?'
Tom wondered aloud.

Jamie pulled the new ammonite fossil out of his pocket. 'The ammonite I gave to Dad was from the Late Cretaceous. I reckon this must be a different ammonite from the Jurassic.'

'I get it,' Tom said. 'Changing the ammonite has changed the time period. It's like your dad said: ammonites really are the key to the past.' He looked sad suddenly. 'But what about Wanna? Will we ever see him again?'

'He'll be waiting for us in the Cretaceous,' Jamie reasoned, stuffing the fossil back in his pocket. 'When we get back to the lighthouse, we'll find the other ammonite. We can still visit him.'

'It won't be the same exploring without Wanna,' Tom said. 'But I guess we have a whole new world to discover. Did you know that the biggest plant eaters that ever lived were in the Jurassic?'

'Yeah, I did.' Jamie grinned, and then looked serious. 'But if there were loads of plant eaters in the Jurassic, wouldn't there have been loads of meat eaters eating them?'

Tom nodded. 'Allosaurs were nearly as big as T-Rex, and just as fierce. And ornitholestes were the size of wolves and hunted in packs. They'd stalk their prey, then creep up and their sharp teeth would—'

Suddenly, the ferns in front of them began to rustle.

'Meat eaters! Hide!' Jamie yelled, hurling

himself into a big pile of dead ferns. Tom
burrowed in beside him. Jamie poked his
finger through the steamy leaf mould and
made a peep-hole.

'What's coming?' Tom whispered.

'The ground didn't shake,' Jamie said,
'so it can't be an allosaurus.'

'Maybe a pack of ornitholestes is
stalking us.' Tom shuddered.

Jamie held his breath as the
ferns rustled fiercely.
What scary dinosaur
would they come
face-to-face with?

CHAPTER 4

A small bony reptilian head poked out of
the ferns.

'Wanna?' Jamie gasped in amazement as
the little Cretaceous dinosaur bounded out of
the Jurassic ferns. Wanna stood on his back
legs, tilted his head to one side, and gazed
down at him with twinkling eyes.

Grunk? It sounded almost like a question.

'It is; it's Wanna!' Tom poked his head out,
pulling pieces of rotting fern out of the neck
of his T-shirt.

Grunk!
Grunk!
Grunk!

Grunk! Grunk! Grunk!

Wanna bobbed his head up and down, grunking ecstatically as Jamie and Tom leapt out of the mound of dead ferns and shook themselves off.

'How did you get here, Wanna?' Jamie
asked. 'You don't belong in the Jurassic.'

'He must be tied to the magic, somehow,'
Tom guessed. 'After all, it is Wanna's fossil
footprints that brought us to Dino World.'

'The Jurassic is even better
now that Wanna's in it,'
Jamie agreed. 'Do you think
he's been here before?'

'It doesn't look like it,'
Tom replied.

Wanna was biting chunks
out of the horsetail ferns and spitting
them out in disgust. He stopped and
looked hopefully at Jamie's backpack.

'Oh, dear,' Jamie said. 'He's hungry and we
didn't pick him any of those stinky gingko
fruits he likes so much.'

'Never mind that,' Tom whispered,
pointing into the sea of tall ferns not far from

41

them. 'I can see a dinosaur.' The tip of a reddish-brown back plate was moving through the greenery. 'It looks like a shark's fin,' he said.

'There weren't any land-sharks in the Jurassic.' Jamie punched Tom on the arm.

Jamie kept his eye on the rustling ferns and caught a glimpse of a small reptilian head the size of Wanna's, with a beaky nose, snuffling through the ferns. There were more of the plate-like fins on the shoulders.

'That could be a stegosaurus!' Tom declared, as the dinosaur moved out of sight among the greenery.

'It could be,' Jamie replied. 'But there was another plated dinosaur: the kentrosaurus. It had spikes on its back as well as the plates near its neck. We have to get a clearer look to be sure.'

They hurried through the ferns, closer to where they spotted the dinosaur.

'It could even be a new sort of dinosaur,' Tom whispered as they crept along. 'People who discover a new dinosaur get to name them. I'd call it tomosaurus.'

'That's not a scientific name,' Jamie retorted. 'Platey-o-saurus would be better.'

Tom thought for a minute. 'How about we call it tomjamosaurus?'

43

'It's a deal.' Jamie grinned. 'Though jatomosaurus sounds good, too.'

Jamie, Tom, and Wanna tracked the dinosaur's trail through the ferns and into a clump of spindly conifer trees.

Suddenly, Wanna gave a grunk and rushed past Jamie, licking his lips. 'Hey, watch where you're going, Wanna!' Jamie called.

Jamie and Tom hurried after their dinosaur friend. Wanna burst out of the ferns into the sunlight.

Suddenly, on the hillside clearing in front of them, there were fifteen reddish-brown speckled dinosaurs, the size of

large trucks,
grazing on a carpet of juicy
ferns. The two rows of diamond-shaped
plates went from their necks all the way
down their domed backs and almost glowed
in the sunshine.

Jamie shaded his eyes. 'They're definitely stegosaurs!'

Tom sighed. 'Too bad we haven't discovered a new dinosaur.'

'But steggies are awesome!' Jamie exclaimed as he flipped open the Fossil Finder and typed in *STEGOSAURUS*. '*THE PLATED LIZARD*,' he read. '*THE SEVENTEEN PLATES DOWN ITS BACK WERE USED FOR DISPLAY. ITS MAIN DEFENCE WAS THE FOUR FEARSOME BONE SPIKES AT THE END OF ITS TAIL.*'

Jamie shut his Fossil Finder and looked at the biggest stegosaur. The spikes on its tail were as long as his arm. They looked as if they were made of steel.

'Wanna's not afraid of them,' Tom said, as their friend trotted into the clearing.

46

The stegosaurs looked up as Wanna passed, and then went back to grazing. 'Let's follow him.'

'Keep out of the way of the steggy spikes,' Jamie warned.

'And don't fall into a steggy cow pat.' Tom chuckled, as they crept up the hill towards the herd of grazing dinosaurs.

The steggies were so close that the boys could hear the grinding of dino teeth and the rumbling and grumbling of dino digestion.

'They're so cool,' Tom whispered.

When the boys were about halfway into the clearing,

a dark shadow fell across the hillside. Jamie looked up to see that the sky was darkening as thunder clouds rolled across it.

A heavy drop of rain fell on Jamie's face, followed by another and another. The steggies began to shuffle away from the grass and into the jungle at the top of the clearing.

'A storm's coming,' Tom said. 'We should find shelter.'

As he spoke, Wanna rushed down and nudged them under a tall broad-leafed fern in the middle of the clearing.

The sky went as dark as night and rain came pelting down. Suddenly, the hillside was lit up by a great sheet of lightning.

'The weather in the Jurassic period is wild!' Tom yelled above the noise of thunder and driving rain. Wanna shivered next to them and jumped a little as another bolt of lightning hit the ground in the clearing.

Jamie peered through the pelting rain and saw one lone stegosaurus left on the hillside. 'Why has that one stayed behind in the rain?' he asked. 'Is there something wrong with it?'

Tom wiped the lenses of his binoculars on his damp T-shirt and focused on the steggy. 'I can see a nest under its belly,' he said. 'It must be a female trying to shelter her eggs from the rain.' Tom handed the binoculars to Jamie.

Jamie zoomed in on the scooped-out nest in the ground. It contained what looked like three mud-covered footballs. Little rivers of

rainwater were streaming down the hill, breaking around the nest.

As Jamie watched, the rain bucketed down even harder, making the river turn into a torrent rushing down the hillside. It rushed around the mother steggy's feet. She peered beneath her belly and brayed in anguish.

Eee-aw, eee-aw, eee-aw!

'What's the matter?' Tom shouted. 'She sounds like a donkey with a megaphone.'

'One of her eggs is washing away,' Jamie yelled. As he watched, the egg began to tumble away from its nest and down the hill. The mother steggy brayed once more, then fell silent and stood her ground.

'She won't leave the nest with the other eggs in it,' Jamie told Tom.

'But that runaway egg might get trampled or lost in the ferns,' Tom said. 'We have to save it!'

CHAPTER 5

SEARCH:

Jamie and Tom hurtled out from the shelter of
the fern, with Wanna grunking and following,
and skidded down the waterlogged hillside
towards the rapidly rolling egg.

Tom stuck out his foot to stop the egg.
'Gotcha!' But the gushing water swept it over
his soggy trainers.

Jamie dived head first at the egg, but the
water running down the hillside changed
direction and swept the slippery egg away
from his outstretched hands. Jamie picked

himself up, spat out a mouthful
of muddy rainwater, and
zig-zagged down the
hillside after it. It was
raining so hard he
could barely see.

Suddenly Wanna
appeared through
the curtain of rain, trying to catch up with
the egg. But he darted right in front of Jamie.

Whump!

Jamie tripped over the little
dinosaur and fell flat on his face
again. He scrambled to his feet
and zig-zagged after
the tumbling egg,
bumping into
Tom and Wanna
who were doing
the same. But every

time the egg
seemed to be within
his grasp, the water
carried it away from him.

'We've got to get below it,'
Tom shouted. 'Block it off!'

Jamie and Tom hurtled
down the hill and flung themselves
sideways across the hillside.

Thunk!

The leathery egg rolled right into Jamie's
stomach. He grabbed it and clutched it to
his chest.

'Great save!' Tom cheered as Jamie struggled to his feet. Rain and mud were dripping from his hair and plopping off the end of his nose. Wanna dashed up, grunking excitedly.

'Let's get out of the rain,' Jamie spluttered, tucking the heavy egg under his arm and heading for the shelter of the trees at the bottom of the hillside clearing.

They crouched beneath a canopy of ferns and examined the rain-washed egg.

'It feels like a leather football,' Tom said. 'No wonder it didn't break.'

Wanna pushed his scaly snout over Jamie's shoulder. *Slurp!* His long reptilian tongue lapped the egg.

'You can't eat it!' Jamie told Wanna, rubbing the dinosaur dribble off the egg with a wet leaf.

In the distance, the mother steggy brayed once and fell silent.

At last, the sky began to lighten and the last raindrops plipped and plopped from the branches of the trees.

'We should put the egg back in the nest now.' Jamie carefully picked it up.

Tom, Jamie, and Wanna cautiously edged up the slippery slope towards the mother steggy. Her tail twitched as she watched them approach.

'Those spikes could spear us like sausages on a stick,'

Jamie whispered
nervously, as they
got nearer. 'But
maybe she knows
we're trying to help.'

The plated lizard was as
big as a bus, a solid domed rock of a reptile.
Jamie was so close that he could reach out
and touch her rubbery scales. He held out
the runaway egg. The mother steggy lowered
her beaky nose and sniffed at it suspiciously.
Her spiky tail began to swish.

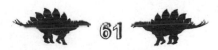

Jamie, Tom, and Wanna froze. Was she going to turn and slash at them?

The mother steggy stared first at the egg then at Tom, Jamie, and Wanna. At last, she blew gently through her nostrils and stepped back from the nest.

'She knows we've rescued her egg,' Jamie whispered as he laid the heavy egg back in the nest where it belonged.

As they watched, the mother steggy bent her head over the nest and gently licked the

eggs. She watched them closely, and the boys watched, too. Jamie gasped as the egg that they'd just rescued shuddered. Then a bulge appeared on one side of the egg.

'It's hatching!' Tom said.

The egg's leathery shell began to rip. A tiny beaky nose pushed its way out of the split, followed by a stumpy little leg.

'It's bright green,' Jamie whispered.

'That will help it hide in the ferns while it's a baby,' Tom said.

The boys and Wanna watched as the baby stegosaurus wriggled and squirmed to free its plump bullfrog-sized body from the egg. At last, it lay on top of the pieces of shell.

'The spikes on its tail are still soft and bent,' Tom murmured. 'Like a baby hedgehog's prickles.'

'And those two rows of tiny bumps are where its plates will grow,' Jamie added. 'It looks like a baby dragon.'

Grunk, grunk, grunk!

Wanna wagged his tail excitedly, then darted forward and gave the new baby dinosaur a slurpy lick.

The baby steggy's tail thumped weakly in reply. Then it raised its head and blinked at the sunshine that was breaking through the clouds.

CHAPTER 6

The mother stegosaurus bent over her baby
and began to lick it clean.

A chorus of rumbling noises erupted around
them. Jamie and Tom jumped to their feet. They
were surrounded by a circle of huge stegosaurs.
'They're welcoming the new arrival,' Tom yelled
above the braying. 'We'd better get out of here
before they make us part of the herd.'

Jamie, Tom, and Wanna squeezed out of the
tightly-packed circle, taking care to dodge the
spikes on the end of the gently swaying tails.

Above them,
a bright rainbow was
forming in the Jurassic sky.

At the edge of the clearing, the boys
stood watching the happy scene until
their damp clothes started to steam in the
baking sunshine and the rainbow began to fade.

'It's time we headed back to the cave,'
Jamie said.

'But it's not on Gingko
Hill, any more,' Tom said. 'We'll
need to make a whole new map.'

'No problem!' Jamie replied.
'We'll call it Gingko Cave.'

The boys followed their trail back down
the hill, through the ferns, to Gingko Cave.
When they got there, Wanna paced nervously
back and forth.

Tom looked worried. 'Wanna hasn't got a nest in the Jurassic. What's he going to do? Should we try to take him back with us?'

'We can't,' Jamie said. 'Everything we try to take back from Dino World turns to dust. He has to stay here.'

'But he'll be scared,' Tom said. 'He doesn't know what's out there.'

'He's a smart dinosaur. Maybe he'll adapt?' Jamie said.

Their dinosaur friend gave a little grunk. He stood back from the cave mouth, lowered his bony head, and began scratching the ground with his feet.

'He's revving up,' Jamie said.

Wanna hurtled head first towards the
rock face at the back of the cave and, the
same instant he would have hit the wall,
he vanished!

'What if he's gone through to our time?'
Tom wondered. 'He'll have turned to dust.
We'll have lost him for ever!'

'That would be terrible.' Jamie frowned. He placed his feet nervously in the muddy version of the fossilized footprints, walking backwards, followed closely by Tom.

'One, two, three, four . . .' Jamie held his breath. 'Five!'

Jamie switched on his torch in the darkness and his heart pounded as he shone his torch on the cave floor. There was no sign of any dust.

'Wanna's safe!' Tom said, sounding relieved.

'He must have gone back home to the Cretaceous,' Jamie replied, as they squeezed back into the smugglers' cave.

'I bet he's curled up in his nest waiting for our next visit to Dino World,' Tom agreed.

The boys hurried back to the lighthouse; the museum was packed with visitors. Jamie's dad was standing by his ammonite exhibit,

smiling broadly as a big group of excited kids
and their parents dug fossils out of the sand.

A young girl dusted off her
fossil and walked over
to the ammonite
display case.

'Mine's from the Jurassic period,' she declared.

'Ah, the Jurassic,' Jamie's dad echoed wistfully. 'It was a golden age for dinosaurs and reptiles of the air and sea. It must have been a very exciting time.'

'You're right, Mr Morgan,' Tom agreed. 'The Jurassic certainly is . . . I mean was . . . a very exciting time.' He nudged Jamie and whispered, 'Hold on to that ammonite, Jamie.'

'Definitely!' Jamie grinned at Tom as he put the Jurassic ammonite safely in his backpack. Now that they knew ammonites were the keys to the past, they could go back to the Late Cretaceous or any other time period. But for now, he couldn't wait to get back to the Jurassic and meet more dinosaurs!

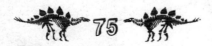

DINOSAUR WORLD

- - - - BOYS' ROUTE

Humungus Waterfall

Massive Canyon

Thick Jungle

Plains

Fin Rock

Jurassic Ocean

Misty Mountains

Gingko Cave

Discovery
Hills

GLOSSARY

Allosaurus(al-oh-sor–us) – a large meat-eating dinosaur at the top of the food chain, it was very tall, over 8.5 metres, and had a distinct horned ridge above its eyes.

Ammonite – an extinct animal with octopus-like legs and often a spiral-shaped shell that lived in the ocean.

Archaeopteryx (ar-kee-op-ter-ix) – the earliest bird capable of flight, with sharp teeth, three clawed fingers, and a long bony tail. Archaeopteryx was not a fussy feeder, eating small animals, plants, and insects.

Brachiosaurus (bra-kee-oh-sor-us) – had a long neck, like a giraffe. This gentle giant loved its greens, munching through 200 kg of plants a day!

Cretaceous (cret-ay-shus) – from about 65 to 150 million years ago, this time period was home to the widest variety of dinosaur and insect life of any period. Birds replaced winged dinosaurs, while in the sea, sharks and rays multiplied.

Jurassic – from about 150 to 200 million years ago, the Jurassic age was warm and humid, with lush jungle cover and great marine diversity. Large dinosaurs ruled on land, while the first birds took to the air.

Kentrosaurus (ken-tro-sor-us) – a slow, plant-eating dinosaur with a double row of six sharp plates down its spine and a spiked tail for self-defence.

Ornitholestes (or-nee-thol-es-tees) – this 'bird robber' was a fast-moving, small, carnivorous dinosaur that probably preyed on small animals and lizards.

Stegosaurus (steg-oh-sor-us) – a large plant-eating dinosaur and a relative of the kentrosaurus, stegosaurus had heavy plated armour and a long row of kite-shaped spikes down its spine, and another row behind its shoulders for defence.

Do you dare
to come into
the water?